Have You Ever Seen a Sneep?

For Olivia and her lovely mum, Lisa
T.P.

For Crista
J.S.

HAVE YOU EVER SEEN A SNEEP?
A PICTURE CORGI BOOK 978 0 552 55698 9

First published in Great Britain by Doubleday,
an imprint of Random House Children's Books
A Random House Group Company

Doubleday edition published 2009
Picture Corgi edition published 2010

1 3 5 7 9 10 8 6 4 2

Text copyright © Tasha Pym, 2009
Illustrations copyright © Joel Stewart, 2009

The right of Tasha Pym and Joel Stewart to be identified as the author
and illustrator of this work has been asserted in accordance
with the Copyright, Designs and Patents Act 1988.

Picture Corgi Books are published by Random House Children's Books,
61–63 Uxbridge Road, London W5 5SA

www.**kidsatrandomhouse**.co.uk
www.**rbooks**.co.uk

Addresses for companies within The Random House Group Limited
can be found at: www.randomhouse.co.uk/offices.htm

THE RANDOM HOUSE GROUP Limited Reg. No. 954009

A CIP catalogue record for this book is available from the British Library.

Printed in China

Have You Ever Seen a SNEEP?

Tasha Pym

Illustrated by
Joel Stewart

PICTURE CORGI

Have you ever set out
   a picnic in a truly
            splendid spot,

turned your back
for just one second . . .

. . . to find a Sneep
has pinched the lot?

Have you ever wanted some quiet,
a little time to read a book,

settled down beneath a tree . . .

. . . to have it
   ruined by a Snook?

Then I bet you've been
down by a stream,
playing on a rope,

swung out
and over the water . . .

. . . and straight down
a Grullock's throat?

Surely you've spied a Knoo and thought,
"Of all the curious things!"

Gone in to take a closer look . . .

. . . to discover
   that it springs?

You simply *must* have been out walking then,
maybe whistling a tune,

just going about your business . . .

. . . then been chased
home by a Loon?

Where you live there are no Grullocks

or Sneeps?

No Snooks?

No Loons?

No Knoo?

Well then, I hope that you
won't mind, because . . .

. . . I'm coming
to live with you!

If you liked *Have You Ever Seen a Sneep?*
then you'll love the adventures of Dexter Bexley:

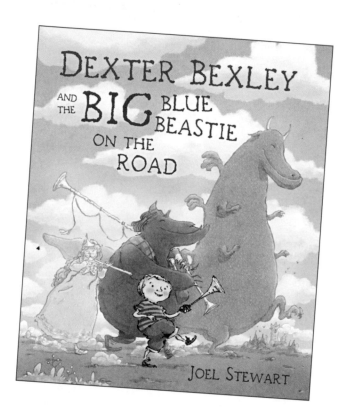